A Giant First-Start Reader

This easy reader contains only 25 different words, repeated often to help the young reader develop word recognition and interest in reading.

Basic word list for *What Time Is It?*

breakfast	it	sing
climb	jump	skip
cook	lunch	sleep
dance	play	swim
dinner	read	time
dream	ride	to
for	run	what
is	school	work
	sew	

What Time Is It?

Written by Judith Grey

Illustrated by Susan Hall

Troll Associates

Library of Congress Cataloging in Publication Data

Grey, Judith.
  What time is it?

    Summary: Demonstrates the proper time for
various activities.
    [1. Time—Fiction.   2. Play—Fiction]   I. Hall,
Susan.   II. Title.
PZ7.G868Wh   [E]   81-5113
ISBN 0-89375-509-5   AACR2
ISBN 0-89375-510-9 (pbk.)

What time is it?

Is it time for breakfast?

Is it time for lunch?

Is it time for dinner?

What time is it?

Is it time to sing?

Is it time to dance?

Is it time to dream?

What time is it?

Is it time to run?

Is it time to swim?

Is it time to ride?

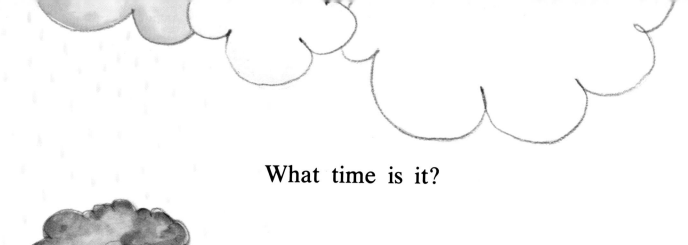

What time is it?

Is it time to skip?

Is it time to jump?

Is it time to climb?

What time is it?

Is it time to play?

Is it time to work?

Is it time for school?

What time is it?

Is it time to sew?

Is it time to cook?

Is it time to sleep?

What time is it?

It is time to read!